Cluckie's
Chicken Pox

Ashley Price Rucker
Author/Illustrator

Published by Scribblers Press
9741 SW 174th Place Road
Summerfield, Florida 34491

Printed by Trinity Press
3190 Reps Miller Road, Suite 360,
Norcross, Georgia 30071

Illustrated by Ashley Price Rucker
Layout by Bridgett Joyce
Text set in Spring Chicken
Printed in U.S.A.

Library of Congress Control Number: 2022921114
Ashley Price Rucker 11/11/2022
Cluckie's Chicken Pox-Varicela de Cluckie - English and Spanish Versions /
Ashley Price Rucker
Summary: Cluckie the chicken's journey of having chicken pox
ISBN: 978-1-950308-49-1

Contact Information
ruckerpartyof5@gmail.com and www.scribblersweb.com

Ordering Information
For ordering this book visit www.scribblersweb.com or Amazon.com

DEDICATION

To our daughter Ashley, we are so very proud of you and your accomplishments. This children's book has been a long desired project to put your high school assignment in print. You have an amazing gift and this little story is just a beginning of what you are destined to do in your life. We thank God for blessing us with you!

Love,
Mom and Dad
Proverbs 3:5-6 KJV

One day Cluckie the chicken was out picking corn with his dad. He spotted a small green worm with red dots all over it.

The worm looked very sick and unhappy. He was
rubbing his back between two corn kernels.

The worm saw Cluckie looking at him, so he asked
Cluckie if he would scratch his back for him?
Cluckie scratched the worm's back,
and went on his way.

Later that night,
Cluckie was laying in his bed,
but couldn't sleep because
red itchy bumps were popping up
all over his body.

He ran to his mom and dad asking why he was itching so much? His mom looked at the red bumps and told him he had chicken pox.

So for the rest of the week,
Cluckie had to stay home from school.

His mom told him not to touch the red bumps,
and keep aloe on them.
Very soon Cluckie was better,
and told all of his friends not to touch
little green worms with red bumps!

THE
END

Varicela de
Cluckie

Ashley Price Rucker
Author/Illustrator

Un día, Cluckie, el pollo, estaba recogiendo maíz con su papá. Vio un pequeño gusano verde con puntos rojos por todas partes.

El gusano parecía muy enfermo e infeliz. Se frotaba la espalda entre dos granos de maíz.

El gusano vio a Cluckie mirándolo, así que le preguntó a Cluckie si le rascaría la espalda. Cluckie rascó la espalda del gusano y siguió su camino.

Más tarde esa noche,
Cluckie estaba acostado en su cama,
pero no podía dormir porque aparecían
protuberancias rojas que le picaban
por todo el cuerpo.

Corrió hacia su mamá y papá preguntando por qué le picaba tanto. Su mamá miró las protuberancias rojas y le dijo que tenía varicela.

Así que durante el resto de la semana, Cluckie tuvo que quedarse en casa y no ir a la escuela.

Su mamá le dijo que no se tocara las protuberancias rojas y que las mantuviera con aloe. ¡Muy pronto, Cluckie mejoró y les dijo a todos sus amigos que no tocaran a los pequeños gusanos verdes con bultos rojos!

EL
FIN

¿Ves a Cluckie?

Made in the USA
Monee, IL
25 November 2022